For Lily

Orchard Books,
95 Madison Avenue, New York, NY 10016

Manufactured in the United States of America
Printed by Barton Press, Inc.
Bound by Horowitz/Rae
The text of this book is set in 18 point Berling.
The illustrations are acrylics reproduced in full color.

1 3 5 7 9 10 8 6 4 2

Library of Congress Cataloging-in-Publication Data
Drawson, Blair.
Mary Margaret's tree / Blair Drawson.
p.   cm.
"A Richard Jackson book"—Half t.p.
Summary: While working so hard to plant her tree, a
young girl imagines herself shrinking and she spends a year
observing nature in the tree's branches.
ISBN 0-531-09521-5. — ISBN 0-531-08871-5 (lib. bdg.)
[1. Trees—Fiction. 2. Nature—Fiction.] I. Title.
PZ7.D7834Mar   1996
[E]—dc20   96-3998

#EFIC 7-9-01

BLAIR DRAWSON

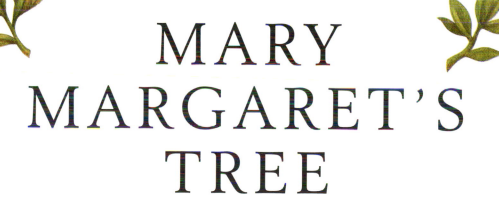

MARY MARGARET'S TREE

ORCHARD BOOKS • NEW YORK

It was spring, and Mary Margaret had

    a tree to plant.

Down in the garden, she dug a hole.

She turned up several stones,

    some tin cans,

    two rusty nails,

    and an old bone.

At night, the sky was full of bright stars
and fireflies.

Digging was hard work.

By the time she was finished, Mary Margaret was

   quite tired.

For some reason, she also felt

   rather small.

What on earth?

    She was shrinking!

But the tree took root

    and sprouted many leaves,

    and grew to become tall

    and magnificent.

Gathering her courage,

    Mary Margaret climbed the mighty trunk.

It was green,

    green,

    green among the leaves!

She made her way to the top of a tall branch.

It was a wonderful thing
    to see the world from on high.

Birds flew back and forth,
    busily building nests.
Strange insects chirped and fluttered,
    chattering in all directions.

Mary Margaret felt snug and happy

inside a large white flower.

"How perfectly lovely," she sighed.

Eggs hatched, and soon the air was filled
　　with the sound of peeping baby birds.
They wanted food!

Mary Margaret was glad
　　that she did not have to
　　eat a worm.

Moths and hooting owls flew

around the moon.

One day there came a flapping of wings,

    and the flower bobbed up and down fearfully.

A huge, hungry woodpecker!

Did it think she was a bug?

Happily, the bird soon realized his mistake,

    and was gone.

Now summer was coming to an end.

The days were getting shorter,

and the nights cooler.

Fall was coming. The leaves were turning color.

It was time for them to go.

Suddenly, a great gust of wind came up,

and Mary Margaret grabbed a leaf

just in time.

She went for a crazy ride!

By chance she flew into a cave.

It was home to some hibernating animals.

There she spent the winter in a deep, peaceful sleep.

Spring arrived at last, and Mary Margaret

    awoke from her slumber.

She began to feel a strange sensation.

Her feet grew roots, and her fingers sent out

    little green shoots.

      Leaves began to appear.

"How very unusual," said Mary Margaret.

Soon there was a brand-new tree,

"Mary Margaret, where are you?"

and the tree was Mary Margaret.

She was being called.

"Come in for dinner now, dear," said her mother.

"You must be hungry."

And Mary Margaret decided

that she really was

very hungry indeed.